Lulu and Lainey

... a Christmas Yarn

by Lois Petren
illustrated by Tanja Russita

Other books by Lois Petren:

Lulu and Lainey … a French Yarn
Lulu and Lainey ... the Lucky Day
Lulu and Lainey ... at the Farm
Lulu and Lainey ... Color with Us

For Alexandra and Ariel

ISBN-13: 978-0-9998099-1-4

"Joyeux Noël, Pierre," Lulu called and ran off.

She stopped to play soccer with her best friend on her way to Grand-mère's apartment and now she was late.

Lulu rushed to Grand-mère's apartment, put her knitting basket down and helped prepare lunch.

They ate sandwiches of grilled ham and cheese and an apple tart ~ yum! Grand-mère's cat, Mimi, prowled the floor looking for crumbs.

Today she planned to knit a Christmas scarf for Pierre with her favorite yarn ~ the lovely green yarn she called Lainey.

After lunch they settled down to knit. Lulu looked for Lainey but it was not in her basket. Suddenly Mimi ran across the floor chasing the ball of yarn.

That cat was always trying to play with Lulu's yarn and today she had succeeded!

Mimi ran down the hall.

Lulu ran after her into the dining room and stopped. Both Lulu and Mimi looked around but did not see Lainey.

"Where did it go?" asked Lulu. "Oh no! How will I make the scarf for Pierre? Is my favorite yarn really lost again?"

With tears in her eyes Lulu went to Grand~mère, who found red yarn that she could use. They worked together all afternoon until Lulu finished knitting the scarf.

Lulu was glad she made such a nice scarf for Pierre, but sad that she lost her favorite ball of yarn again.

She kissed Grand~mère "Adieu" and promised to return with her family for dinner on Christmas Eve.

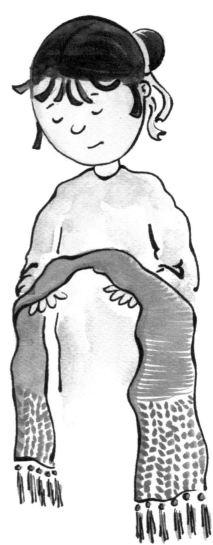

Lulu did not stay sad for long. It was almost
Christmas and everyone was in high
spirits. Carolers were singing
on Paris street corners.

Houses and shops were beautifully decorated.
Children were hoping Père Noël
would leave treats in their
shoes on Christmas Eve.

Finally Christmas Eve arrived - the weather was cold and everyone thought it would snow.

Lulu's mother baked a bûche de Noël while Lulu and her little brother, Bertie, helped make the decorations.

The cake looked just like a log sitting in the forest. It had chocolate frosting and the decorations were leaves and mushrooms made of sweet almond paste.

It was fun to make the shapes - like playing with clay.

Lulu was excited because she and her brother would sleep at Grand~mère's apartment on Christmas Eve.

Lulu hoped Père Noël would find her shoes sitting on the hearth and fill them with treats.

At dinnertime the family walked to Grand-mère's apartment, admiring the decorations along the way.

Grand-mère's apartment was beautifully decorated with lights, holly and a huge Christmas tree next to her fireplace.

The holiday meal was delicious but the best part was when the bûche de Noël was presented and everyone got a big slice.

Later that evening Lulu and Bertie set their shoes out on the hearth for Père Noël and then settled down to dream of Christmas treats.

Mimi prowled the apartment while they slept. She could
see the Christmas tree with its decorations through the
glass door.

Mimi went under the china cabinet in the dining room. It was dark.

When she reached the wall she pushed against an object that was soft and fuzzy. She remembered having lots of fun with something like that.

She pushed it out from under the cabinet.

It was Lainey!

She started to bat the ball of yarn around, chasing it like a mouse. At the door to the parlor, she suddenly stopped.

All the lights were twinkling!

There was a man with black boots, a big red coat with fur trim and a long white beard sticking out from under a red hood.

Père Noël saw the cat with the yarn in her mouth and stopped.

He quickly reached down, grabbed the yarn and then closed the door behind him. He knew exactly where to put it ~ in Lulu's shoe.

Then he disappeared up the chimney. Mimi scampered away.

Christmas morning dawned and Paris had a lovely coating of fresh snow. Lulu and Bertie didn't notice as they ran to the parlor to see what waited for them.

Their shoes were filled with holiday treats. And Lainey was there in Lulu's shoe!

She stopped in front of her shoes and let out a cheer of happiness to see her favorite yarn again.

Later that day Lulu and Bertie ran outside to play in the snow with their friends.

Pierre proudly wore the new red scarf that Lulu had knit for him.

When it was dinnertime they called "Joyeux Noël" to each other and everyone headed home for hot cocoa and their Christmas dinners.

Once again Lainey was safely tucked away in Lulu's knitting basket.

"Joyeux Noël!"

Everyone wondered how Lainey got in Lulu's shoe.

Only Mimi knew ~ and Père Noël, of course.

I hope you enjoyed this book.

Be sure to visit http://www.loisapetren.com to get free coloring
pages and learn more about the world of Lulu and Lainey.

CPSIA information can be obtained
at www.ICGtesting.com
Printed in the USA
LVHW07*1757090718
583160LV00026B/365/P